A Carol for Christmas

Ann Tompert • *illustrated by Laura Kelly*

Simon & Schuster Books for Young Readers

AUTHOR'S NOTE

Many legends have grown around the origin of "Silent Night," which Joseph Mohr and Franz Gruber wrote on December 24, 1818, for the Christmas Eve celebration at the Church of Saint Nicholas. The story told in this book is based on the one most often heard.

After its initial presentation, the hymn became immensely popular in Germany and Austria. By 1838 it was included in various hymnbooks and had started its journey around the world. Today it is sung in nearly one hundred different languages.

The Church of Saint Nicholas in Oberndorf, Austria, was moved to higher ground after being ravaged by floods in 1913. In its place the townspeople erected a small, octagonal chapel decorated with stained-glass windows honoring Joseph Mohr and Franz Gruber, a replica of which has been erected in Frankenmuth, Michigan. For many years, the townspeople of Oberndorf have reenacted in the chapel the events that inspired the writing of the song from heaven, "Silent Night."

SIMON & SCHUSTER BOOKS FOR YOUNG READERS
An imprint of Simon & Schuster Children's Publishing Division, 1230 Avenue of the Americas, New York, New York 10020. Text copyright © 1994 by Ann Tompert. Illustrations copyright © 1994 by Laura Kelly.
All rights reserved including the right of reproduction in whole or in part in any form. Simon & Schuster Books for Young Readers is a trademark of Simon & Schuster. Printed in the United States of America. The text of this book is set in 14 pt. Garamond No. 3. The illustrations are rendered in watercolors.
10 9 8 7 6 5 4 3 2

Printed on recycled paper

Library of Congress Cataloging-in-Publication Data
Tompert, Ann.   A carol for Christmas / Ann Tompert ; illustrated by Laura Kelly. — 1st ed.
p.   cm.   Summary: Relates the important part hungry mice might have played in the creation of the Christmas carol "Silent Night." ISBN 0-02-789402-9 [1. Mohr, Joseph, 1792–1848.   Stille Nacht, heilige Nacht—Fiction.
2. Mice—Fiction.   3. Christmas—Fiction.]   I. Kelly, Laura (Laura C.), ill.   II. Title.   PZ7.T598Car
1994   [E]—dc20   93-9039

For Christa and Yvonne,
friends for all seasons
—A. T.

I survived Art and Punishment
with John Lincoln. I remain
forever grateful for his skill as an
artist and a teacher.
—L. K.

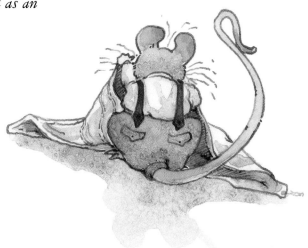

It happened long ago in the Church of Saint Nicholas in Oberndorf, a small town in Austria. I lived there with my mother and father and seventeen younger brothers and sisters.

Although we had always been poor, we'd had enough to eat until the hard winter of 1818. Food became so scarce that our family was reduced to making soup out of bits of leather from the connections of the church organ keys.

Of course the church organist soon discovered what was happening. "Those mice are ruining the organ," I overheard him complain to the pastor one day. "We must get rid of them."

"Gretel," said the pastor. "She's the best mouser in all Oberndorf. I'll borrow her for a week. That should solve the problem."

The next day Gretel's reign of terror against us began. Relentlessly she sniffed about the doorways of our nooks and crannies and patrolled the area around the organ. If her fierce green eyes caught sight of a mouse, she pounced upon it like the snap of a trap.

Fear squeezed my heart every time my father and I made our daily expeditions. "We're sure to be captured by that cruel Gretel," I said to my father one day. "Then who will take care of our family?"

"I don't know, Jeremy," he said, sighing. "Our only hope is to find food elsewhere. But where or how, I have no idea."

I had no idea, either. But then, early in the afternoon of Christmas Eve, I was scurrying along a wall near the church organ when I heard voices. It was the organist and the pastor, inspecting the organ.

The organist threw up his hands. "It's hopeless," he said.

"We must have music at the midnight mass tonight," said the pastor.

"Trying to play this organ is worse than playing my guitar with a broken string," said the organist.

"Your guitar!" exclaimed the pastor. "Why can't you play that?"

"No! No!" protested the organist. "That would never do. Christmas music is too majestic for a guitar."

While I listened, a familiar smell reached my nose. Cheese! I couldn't remember when I had last tasted cheese. My whiskers twitched. My mouth watered. Sniffing the air, I edged forward. Then I flashed across the floor like a lightning streak and followed the smell up the back of the pastor's greatcoat and into a pocket. Luckily the pastor and the organist were so busy talking that they didn't notice my invasion.

After basking in the tantalizing aroma of cheese, which filled the pocket, I explored every inch without finding a crumb. There was cheese here once, I told myself. What had happened to it? Burning tears pushed against my eyelids. But then I reasoned that more cheese might find its way into the pocket, so I decided to wait and see what happened.

As I made myself comfortable, I again became aware of voices.

"I'm glad you understand," said the pastor. "Now, since we have no Christmas music suitable for a guitar, let's compose something. I'll write the words if you'll set them to music." The organist agreed.

The next minute we were moving. I held my breath and clung to a thread in the pocket with shaking paws. Where were we going? I wondered. For a moment I considered escaping, but then I remembered my starving family.

The click of the pastor's boots on the floor echoed in the empty church. A few moments later, a door opened and closed. The pastor's boots crunched in the snow. Icy air seeped into the pocket. I shivered. My teeth chattered. Surely I will freeze to death, I thought.

The pastor stamped his feet. Another door opened and closed. My dark prison lurched about like a ship on a stormy sea. I dug my paws in deeper, closed my eyes, and held my breath.

When I thought that I would lose my grip, fly out of the pocket, and be dashed to the ground, we stopped moving. My fast-beating heart sounded like a drum. I prayed that the pastor wouldn't hear it and discover me. I waited for several minutes.

When nothing happened, I peered out. The coat was on a hook. I looked around the room and found the pastor sitting at his desk, holding Gretel. He made a few scratches on some paper with a pen. Then he gazed at a picture of a mother and father looking with adoring eyes at their child, who lay on some hay in a box. The pastor shook his head, sighed, and scratched on the paper some more. He shook his head and sighed again.

"It's useless," he cried, throwing down his pen. "I need a miracle."

Well, I thought, I need a miracle, too, if I'm to save my family. I started to climb out of the pocket, intending to forage for food. A pounding at the door startled me. The pastor jumped up. Back into the pocket I dove, and collapsed at the bottom. As I lay there trembling, I heard the door open. I peeked out and saw a woman shrouded in snow.

"Come in. Come in," the pastor urged.

"No," said the woman in a breathless voice. "I must be getting home. I've been away since early morning."

As I watched impatiently for an opportunity to escape, I listened to the woman. With words tumbling over one another, she told the pastor that she had assisted in the birth of a child in a deserted cottage deep in the forest. "The one where Hans, the woodcutter, used to live," she said. "The father came here to Oberndorf a few weeks ago to work in the salt mines."

"Yes, yes, I know," said the pastor. "That old hut was the only place he could find to live."

"The mother was hoping that you would visit them and give your blessing," she said.

"I'm busy getting something ready for our midnight mass tonight," said the pastor.

"Tomorrow, then?" asked the woman.

The pastor was silent for a moment. "I'll go now," he said. "Maybe the walk will clear my head."

It was snowing when the pastor stepped out into the street. I poked my head out, looking for a chance to escape. It was hopeless. Everywhere people were hurrying around in the snow-mantled town. The pastor stopped often to greet someone. And there were several lean, hungry-looking cats prowling about. When one tagged after us, making a dreadful racket with his meowing, I sank back into my pocket-prison. There I lay, trembling. Would I be discovered?

We reached the edge of the forest at last. This will be a good time to escape, I thought. But then I realized I was too far from the church. How would I find my way home?

The only sound now was the crunching of the pastor's boots in the snow. At first we moved quickly. But before long we slowed to a crawl. I was cold. My paws were like clumps of ice. Several times the pastor stumbled over rocks and fallen limbs hidden by the deep snow. And I nearly tumbled into the snow because I could barely hold on with my numb paws.

Why, oh, why did I ever leave home? I moaned over and over to myself as I huddled in a corner of my pocket-prison. I was sure that we were lost. But the pastor struggled on until we reached the woodcutter's hut.

There we found the young mother, bundled in blankets, napping beside the fire. The young father was bending over the cradle, smiling at their newborn child. I caught my breath. How like the picture on the pastor's wall they looked! I gazed on the scene with wondering eyes. A warm glow flowed through me. I was no longer cold and miserable. And I knew that somehow I would succeed in my task.

"A Christmas crèche," the pastor murmured as he stomped the snow from his boots.

"You *did* come," said the young mother, waking up and smiling wanly.

"We were afraid you'd be too busy," said the father.

"I'm never too busy to bless a beautiful Christmas baby," said the pastor, leaning over the cradle. He made the sign of the cross and murmured a few words. Then the father knelt beside the mother while the pastor blessed them. As they rose, the father put his arms around the mother, and both looked lovingly at the infant.

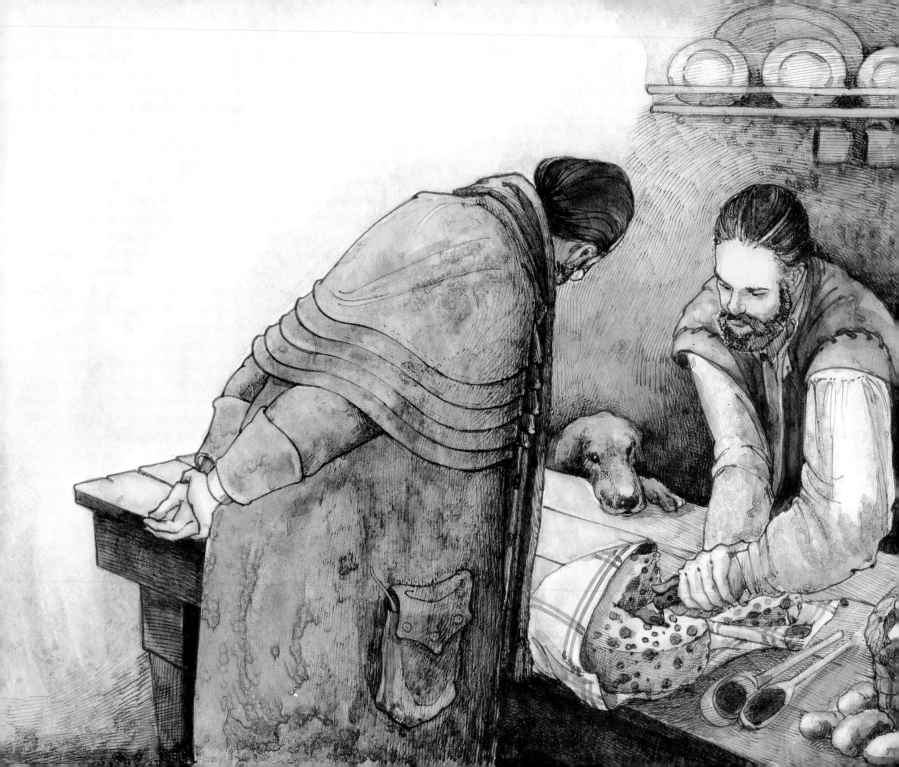

"Won't you stay for supper?" asked the mother.

"It's late," said the pastor. "I must be getting back."

"You must take something to eat along the way," said the father, cutting two hunks from a round of cheese.

I ducked when the pastor slipped one piece into the pocket.

"We're truly grateful that you came," the father called after us when we set out for home.

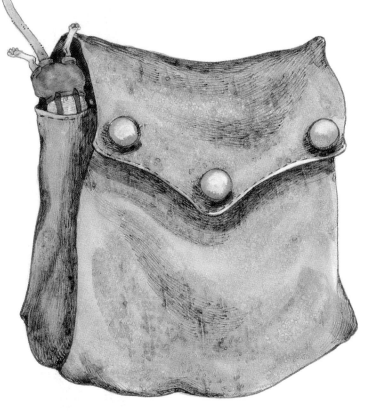

Then I forgot everything while I feasted on cheese until I couldn't nibble another bite. After filling my haversack, I looked out. Snow was no longer falling. The sun had set. But the air felt warmer. A full moon was rising. We skimmed over the snow. The way that had seemed so difficult before seemed easy now.

The pastor stopped and gazed at the star-sprinkled sky. "How bright the night is!" he exclaimed. "And how silent."

After that he walked more slowly, muttering to himself. I slipped to the bottom of the pocket, curled up in a corner, and fell asleep. I don't know how long I slept. I was awakened by a voice demanding, "Where have you been?"

When I peeked out I found that we were back in the pastor's house. The organist was there with his guitar.

"In Bethlehem," said the pastor.

Then I was catapulted through the air. I clung desperately to my haversack with one paw and to the pocket with the other. I landed on something hard. My head spun around and around. When it cleared I peeked out again. The pastor had thrown his coat onto the bench by the fireplace. He was at his desk, scratching furiously with his pen.

"Here," he said some minutes later, handing the paper to the organist. "It's our Christmas song."

The organist strummed his guitar and began to hum a melody as he looked at the words. "It's beautiful," he said. "A song from heaven."

While the organist worked, I tried several times to escape. But Gretel was there to thwart my efforts. Thank goodness the cat would be going home with her owner after the midnight mass.

I was still trapped in my pocket-prison when the town clock struck eleven. Then the pastor put on the greatcoat, and he and the organist hurried to the church. There, amid the confusion of crowds of people gathering for the midnight mass, I was able to escape at last.

I found my family in mourning, thinking I had met my end under the claws of the wicked Gretel. Great was their rejoicing upon my return. Tears of sorrow turned to tears of joy as they nibbled cheese while I told of my adventures.

Just as I'd finished, the sound of guitar music drifted into the room. Motioning my family to follow, I crept into the church. We listened, spellbound, as the organist played his guitar while he and the pastor sang.

Silent night, holy night,
All is calm, all is bright;
Round yon Virgin Mother and Child,
Holy Infant so tender and mild,
Sleep in heavenly peace,
Sleep in heavenly peace.

Silent night, holy night,
Shepherds quake at the sight;
Glories stream from heaven afar;
Heavenly host sing Alleluia!
Christ the Savior is born,
Christ the Savior is born.

Silent night, holy night,
Son of God, love's pure light.
Radiant beams from Thy holy face,
With the dawn of redeeming grace,
Jesus, Lord, at Thy birth,
Jesus, Lord, at Thy birth.

Since that memorable night, that carol has become very popular. I would not be surprised if someday it is heard around the world every year at Christmastime. I wonder if anyone will remember that it was because of us mice at Saint Nicholas that the song was written.